POEMS
for Children

pictures by GYO FUJIKAWA

TITLE IVB

PLATT & MUNK, PUBLISHERS/New York
A Division of Grosset & Dunlap

HOLMAN

ANNIE'S GARDEN

In little Annie's garden
    Grew all sorts of posies;
There were pinks, and mignonette,
    And tulips, and roses.

Sweet peas, and morning glories,
    A bed of violets blue,
And marigolds, and asters,
    In Annie's garden grew.

There the bees went for honey,
    And the hummingbirds, too;
And there the pretty butterflies
    And the ladybirds flew.

And there among her flowers,
    Every bright and pleasant day,
In her own pretty garden
    Little Annie went to play.

Eliza Lee Follen

THE MONTHS

January brings the snow,
Makes our feet and fingers glow.

February brings the rain,
Thaws the frozen lake again.

May brings flocks of pretty lambs,
Skipping by their fleecy dams.

June brings tulips, lilies, roses,
Fills the children's hands with posies.

Warm September brings the fruit;
Sportsmen then begin to shoot.

Fresh October brings the pheasant;
Then to gather nuts is pleasant.

March brings breezes loud and shrill,
Stirs the dancing daffodil.

April brings the primrose sweet,
Scatters daisies at our feet.

Hot July brings cooling showers,
Apricots and gillyflowers.

August brings the sheaves of corn;
Then the harvest home is borne.

Dull November brings the blast,
When the leaves are whirling fast.

Chill December brings the sleet,
Blazing fires and Christmas treat.

Sara Coleridge

WINTER

Bread and milk for breakfast,
  And woolen frocks to wear,
And a crumb for robin redbreast
  On the cold days of the year.

Christina Rossetti

CHRISTMAS BELLS

I heard the bells on Christmas Day
Their old, familiar carols play,
    And wild and sweet
    The words repeat
Of peace on earth, good will to men!

And thought how, as the day had come,
The belfries of all Christendom
    Had rolled along
    The unbroken song
Of peace on earth, good will to men!

Till, ringing, singing, on its way,
The world revolved from night to day,
    A voice, a chime,
    A chant sublime
Of peace on earth, good will to men!

              Henry Wadsworth Longfellow

RAIN IN SUMMER

How beautiful is the rain!
After the dust and heat,
In the broad and fiery street,
In the narrow lane,
How beautiful is the rain!
How it clatters along the roofs,
Like the tramp of hoofs!

How it gushes and struggles out
From the throat of the overflowing spout!
Across the windowpane
It pours and pours;
And swift and wide,
With a muddy tide,
Like a river down the gutter roars
The rain, the welcome rain!

Henry Wadsworth Longfellow

MINNIE AND WINNIE

Minnie and Winnie
   Slept in a shell.
Sleep, little ladies!
   And they slept well.

Pink was the shell within,
   Silver without;
Sounds of the great sea
   Wandered about.

Sleep, little ladies!
   Wake not soon!
Echo on echo
   Dies to the moon.

Two bright stars
   Peeped into the shell.
"What are they dreaming of?
   Who can tell?"

Started a green linnet
   Out of the croft;
Wake, little ladies!
   The sun is aloft.

                    Alfred, Lord Tennyson

THE DUEL

The gingham dog and the calico cat
Side by side on the table sat;
"Twas half-past twelve, and (what do you think!)
Nor one nor t'other had slept a wink!
    The old Dutch clock and the Chinese plate
    Appeared to know as sure as fate
There was going to be a terrible spat.
    (I wasn't there; I simply state
    What was told to me by the Chinese plate!)

The gingham dog went, "Bow-wow-wow!"
And the calico cat replied, "Mee-ow!"
The air was littered, an hour or so,
With bits of gingham and calico,
    While the old Dutch clock in the chimney-place
    Up with its hands before its face,
For it always dreaded a family row!
    (Now mind; I'm only telling you
    What the old Dutch clock declares is true!)

The Chinese plate looked very blue,
And wailed, "Oh, dear! what shall we do!"
But the gingham dog and the calico cat
Wallowed this way and tumbled that,
    Employing every tooth and claw
    In the awfullest way you ever saw—
And oh! how the gingham and calico flew!
    (Don't fancy I exaggerate—
    I got my news from the Chinese plate!)

THE MILK JUG
(The Kitten Speaks)

The Gentle Milk Jug blue and white
    I love with all my soul;
She pours herself with all her might
    To fill my breakfast bowl.

All day she sits upon the shelf,
    She does not jump or climb—
She only waits to pour herself
    When 'tis my suppertime.

And when the Jug is empty quite,
    I shall not mew in vain,
The Friendly Cow all red and white,
    Will fill her up again.

Oliver Herford

Next morning, where the two had sat
They found no trace of dog or cat;
And some folks think unto this day
That burglars stole that pair away!
    But the truth about the cat and pup
    Is this: they ate each other up!
Now what do you really think of that!
    (The old Dutch clock it told me so,
    And that is how I came to know.)
Eugene Field

THE OWL AND THE PUSSYCAT

The Owl and the Pussycat went to sea
  In a beautiful pea-green boat;
They took some honey, and plenty of money
  Wrapped up in a five-pound note.
The Owl looked up to the stars above,
  And sang to a small guitar,
"O lovely Pussy, O Pussy, my love,
  What a beautiful Pussy you are,
    You are,
    You are!
  What a beautiful Pussy you are!"

Pussy said to the Owl, "You elegant fowl,
  How charmingly sweet you sing!
Oh, let us be married; too long we have
    tarried:
  But what shall we do for a ring?"
They sailed away, for a year and a day,
  To the land where the bong-tree grows,
And there in a wood a Piggy-wig stood,
  With a ring at the end of his nose,
    His nose,
    His nose,
  With a ring at the end of his nose.

"Dear Pig, are you willing to sell for one
    shilling
  Your ring?" Said the Piggy, "I will.",
So they took it away, and were married next
    day
  By the turkey who lives on the hill.
They dined on mince and slices of quince,
  Which they ate with a runcible spoon;
And hand in hand, on the edge of the sand,
  They danced by the light of the moon,
    The moon,
    The moon,
  They danced by the light of the moon.

Edward Lear

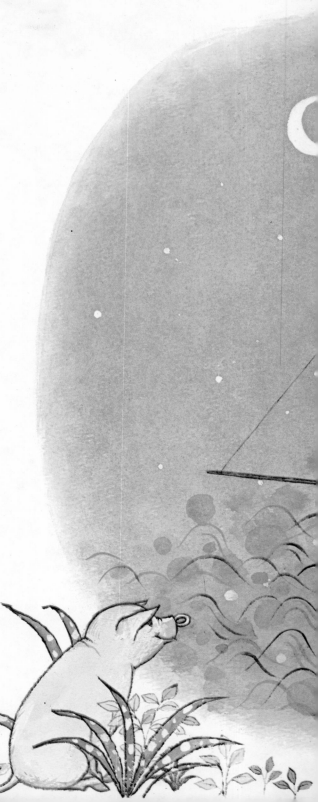

A BOY'S SONG

Where the pools are bright and deep,
Where the gray trout lies asleep,
Up the river, and over the lea,
That's the way for Billy and me.

Where the blackbird sings the latest,
Where the hawthorne blooms the sweetest,
Where the nestlings chirp and flee,
That's the way for Billy and me.

Where the mowers mow the cleanest,
Where the hay lies thick and greenest;
There to trace the homeward bee,
That's the way for Billy and me.

Where the hazel bank is steepest,
Where the shadow falls the deepest,
Where the clustering nuts fall free,
That's the way for Billy and me.

James Hogg

DAFFODILS

I wandered lonely as a cloud
That floats on high o'er vales and hills,
When all at once I saw a crowd—
A host of golden daffodils
Beside the lake, beneath the trees,
Fluttering and dancing in the breeze.

Continuous as the stars that shine
And twinkle on the Milky Way,
They stretched in never-ending line
Along the margin of a bay:
Ten thousand saw I, at a glance,
Tossing their heads in sprightly dance.

The waves beside them danced, but they
Out-did the sparkling waves in glee:
A poet could not but be gay,
In such a jocund company:
I gazed—and gazed—but little thought
What wealth the show to me had brought:

For oft, when on my couch I lie
In vacant or in pensive mood,
They flash upon that inward eye
Which is the bliss of solitude;
And then my heart with pleasure fills,
And dances with the daffodils.

William Wordsworth

THE CROCODILE

How doth the little crocodile
    Improve his shining tail,
And pour the waters of the Nile
    On every golden scale!

How cheerfully he seems to grin,
    How neatly spreads his claws,
And welcomes little fishes in,
    With gently smiling jaws!

Lewis Carroll

QUEEN MAB

A little fairy comes at night,
Her eyes are blue, her hair is brown,
With silver spots upon her wings,
And from the moon she flutters down.

She has a little silver wand,
And when a good child goes to bed
She waves her hand from right to left,
And makes a circle round its head.

And then it dreams of pleasant things,
Of fountains filled with fairy fish,
And trees that bear delicious fruit,
And bow their branches at a wish:

Of arbors filled with dainty scents
From lovely flowers that never fade;
Bright flies that glitter in the sun,
And glowworms shining in the shade:

And talking birds with gifted tongues,
For singing songs and telling tales,
And pretty dwarfs to show the way
Through fairy hills and fairy dales.

Thomas Hood

WHAT ROBIN TOLD

How do robins build their nests?
   Robin Redbreast told me—
First a wisp of yellow hay
In a pretty round they lay;

Then some shreds of downy floss,
Feathers, too, and bits of moss,
Woven with a sweet, sweet song,
This way, that way, and across;
   THAT'S what Robin told me.

Where do robins hide their nests?
   Robin Redbreast told me—
Up among the leaves so deep,
Where the sunbeams rarely creep,
Long before the leaves are gold,
Bright-eyed stars will peep and see
Baby robins—one, two, three;
   THAT'S what Robin told me.

George Cooper

THREE LITTLE TREES

A dear little secret,
As sweet as could be,
The breeze told one day
To the glad apple tree.
The breeze told the apple,
The apple the plum,
The plum told the pear,
"Robin Redbreast has come."